Past the Layered Stones

by Ivaylo R. Shmilev

Errors are excepted. This is a work of fiction. Any resemblance to actual events, locales, organisations, persons living or dead, etc. is entirely coincidental.

Text set in Liberation Serif.
Further information: https://fedorahosted.org/liberation-fonts/

Cover image background produced using Chaoscope.
Further information: http://chaoscope.org/faq.htm

Cover image uses Luxi fonts. Luxi fonts copyright © 2001 by Bigelow & Holmes Inc. Luxi font instruction code copyright © 2001 by URW++ GmbH. All Rights Reserved. Luxi is a registered trademark of Bigelow & Holmes Inc. Permission is hereby granted, free of charge, to any person obtaining a copy of these Fonts and associated documentation files (the "Font Software"), to deal in the Font Software, including without limitation the rights to use, copy, merge, publish, distribute, sublicense, and/or sell copies of the Font Software, and to permit persons to whom the Font Software is furnished to do so.
Licence & further information:
http://www.fontsquirrel.com/license/Luxi-Serif

Available from Amazon.com, CreateSpace.com, and other retail outlets.
ISBN-13: 978-1541241022
ISBN-10: 1541241029

Dedications

To my mother, father and sister;

to my good friends;

and to those whom we long to embrace
but who are forever gone beyond our reach.

Contents

Past the Layered Stones

The Collected Poetry of
Jared Quieton Ilyief Vile

by Jared Q. I. Vile

edited by A. E. Arhangelskaya-Ing,
A. Vile and R. Gev

with an introduction by A. E. Arhangelskaya-Ing,
an academic analysis by F. J. Bloownt and an afterword by A. Vile

Library Data

Full title: Past the Layered Stones: The Collected Poetry of
Jared Quieton Ilyief Vile

Author: Jared Quieton Ilyief Vile (2877 - 2942 [presumed])

Original release date: 4258.05.24

Editors: A. E. Arhangelskaya-Ing, A. Vile and R. Gev

Introduction: A. E. Arhangelskaya-Ing

Notes: Includes an academic analysis by F. J. Bloownt, an
afterword by A. Vile and an addendum.

UHCN: 324.798.237.498.57-123.761.873.468.74-
827.463.784.638.00

Introduction to the Collected Poetry of Jared Quieton Ilyief Vile

by A. E. Arhangelskaya-Ing

What you're holding in your hands is both the sweet fruit of lucky circumstances and a labour of love.

The strange and, as many believe, rather short life of Jared Quieton Ilyief Vile ended long before his poetry could see the light of day. Born in the last quarter of the 29th century (in 2877), Jared Vile disappeared without a trace roughly three years after the start of the First Systemwide Sol War. In his public life, he was known as a sturdy opponent to the Ultracontinentals, as a popular speaker, an unpublished poet and a fledgling musician. His works, mostly essays on current topics, were among the many burnt or otherwise destroyed by the Ultracon regime. As a minor political figure in the struggles of the early 30th century, Jared Vile earned the respect of his peers for his slow, practised and persuasive manner of public speech and his similarly calm and confident, though politically and historically well-informed, oppositional stance. Virtually all records of his public engagements have disappeared and most of the information we currently have on him has come across the gulf of time via witnesses who survived the brutalities of the Ultracon regime, chief among them, of course, Jared Vile's relatives and friends.

The person who approached me with this extraordinary find, his great-great-granddaughter Andonia Vile, represents one of the few remaining living links to that time of unprecedented turmoil and horror. Last year, while cleaning out an old family house in New Hellven on Mars, she happened upon a small strongbox. Surprisingly, the strongbox was not locked or secured in any way; it was a slightly battered, comparatively flat metallic object lying unobtrusively among other flat objects – ancient books and magazines and other papers. In it, Andonia found a journal-like notebook, carefully arranged printouts and several hand-written manuscript pages. The discovery, she quickly determined, comprised two separate and exceedingly valuable objects: Jared

Vile's own diary for the period (roughly) from 2928 to 2936 and the draft of a collection of poetry, with poems ordered into larger parts or, probably, cycles. The journal gave her clues about the printed and hand-written manuscript papers, but the various paper materials themselves had begun to decompose, despite having been relatively well preserved in the strongbox for so many centuries, and so were difficult to read and comprehend. Andonia told me, when we first met and spoke about this, that the box had almost been sent for recycling along with the old books. Perhaps it was her thoroughness, intuition, or the leisurely summer – or maybe all of these combined – that made her take the time and look properly into a number of old cartons destined for the recycler. She realised the lucky circumstance of her discovery very soon; the find posed an unexpected problem though. Andonia immediately decided to publish the collection and would have liked to do so on her own but lacked the necessary skills in restoration and linguistics, as well as the needed connections to helpful specialists in this area of literary archaeology and anthropology.

Needless to say, I was exhilarated and immensely grateful that she selected me to work with on this publication. Being approached with such a project instead of a well-established name in the field like Salana Perushi, Ojdamnof Gryk or Bernard Ftumbasupo (greetings, colleagues and teachers!) gave me, in turn, a week-long epinephrine rush, so I contacted friends and colleagues to discuss restoration options in detail and, by quietly sharing the nature of the discovery, to slow down my own imagination's wild spinning and focus on the tasks ahead. An old and very good friend of mine, Romonu Gev, agreed to take time off its production engagements and assist us in the work. Romonu was, in many ways, one of the best choices for this undertaking: it is busy with materials production and some construction work on new settlements in nearby systems so it has easy access to enormously useful production facilities. What's more, it has extensive knowledge of space mining and materials science, which came in extremely handy when we decided to reveal this truly astonishing find to the world by publishing it on excellent paper imitation, the way Jared Vile himself would have likely wanted to release his work back in the day. Romonu put in an upstanding effort and created a remixed, updated and rather efficient imitation paper recipe based on current gigaorganics combined with common and abundant asteroid ore products. Its help with the scanning and character recognition of faded texts as well as the deciphering of older, more archaic expressions was inestimable. Both Andonia and I owe it a solid debt of gratitude.

The three of us laboured for several months on this project, frequently hid from families and friends, ignored pleasurable and important events and did go sleepless through a number of nights (our machine friend Romonu required, by nature, little rest); however, the actual fruit of our labours – the physical object we still, after so many millennia, fondly call a book – and the fact that we now reveal it as Andonia intended, and perhaps her great-great-grandfather Jared did as well, are the perfect repayment for the loving effort we invested. To put this in the simplest words I could find: it was wonderful that it happened, and it was very much worth it to put in the necessary sweat.

I know, nevertheless, that some of you are already asking yourselves: why not also publish the journal Andonia Vile discovered? It must contain even more curious and scientifically relevant insights about the life and times of Jared Q. I. Vile. In fact, simple and quickly composed journal entries will unveil much more information about the person and the historical times than the poetry written by that person because the immediacy and tangible relevance of diary writing reflect the world more transparently than the twisting and turning multi-dimensional lanes of poetic expression. Unfortunately, Andonia decided against this, mainly due to the strongly personal nature of the entries. What I am at liberty to say about the diary boils down to the following: Jared Vile's notes mostly concern his immediate family and their mundane troubles, an illness of his – he suffered a rather dangerous form of cancer and defeated it with the help of a long and arduous (for that time) nano-machine regimen – as well as, very rarely, his creative process and the poetry collection he prepared. The diary refers to another journal on several occasions. It's possible that the other journal might include much more intriguing information on Jared and his life; its status, however, is completely unknown. Andonia is currently attempting to locate it (or at least find any remaining clues about it) by scouring all available family accommodations and archives. As of this writing, the search has not been successful.

This may well mean that the only record of Jared Vile's social and political life we will ever have is contained within the pages of his poetry. In such situations, the ancient wisdom still holds: it's better to have something than nothing at all. My partners-in-restoration-crime (just joking, naturally!) and I resolved to keep the poetry as close as possible to its original style and only changed words and phrases when they would both fit the diverse rhythm patterns he employed – according to Jared's own notes, he always strove to write poetry that's to be read out loud – and simultaneously preserve the meaning as strictly as linguistically feasible. In this process, Romonu suggested tens, hundreds and at times thousands of options, whereas the final decisions were taken by the three of us together, with more weight given to Andonia's intuition due to her intimate knowledge of the rediscovered journal. We changed neither the order nor the seven parts into which Jared originally arranged the poems. The title of the collection, *Past the Layered Stones*, also reflects his wish and plan. The only additions to Jared Vile's design are this introduction, well-known cultural critic F. J. Bloownt's serious and deeply analytical essay on the collection and Andonia Vile's afterword. We would all like to express our gratitude to Mr Bloownt who stepped in to support us and lend this endeavour an amount of academic credibility at very short notice.

Last but certainly not least, I am excited to finally have this project completed and released to the public. I believe that our work might shed some light on a dark but, ultimately, tremendously significant period of our distant history. There is of course, in certain circles, speculation that Jared Vile did not really vanish without a trace but rather altered his appearance and, later, became known as the revolutionary Joseph Astas Kir Demeter. History books agree that Joseph Demeter, also variously known as Joe AK, Joey K, JAK, Jack D, JD, or any of the thousand other monikers he and others used, proved to be one of the most determined and effective opponents of the Ultracon regime; some historians credit his organising genius and guerrilla actions as major factors in the downfall of the Ultracontinentals almost fifty years after they established themselves in power and began to slowly drag the entire system into unprecedentedly devastating war. (Demeter disappeared completely, too, around the beginning of the fourth millennium and approximately one decade after direct participatory democracy was finally restored.) Jared Vile's poetry collection will quite likely disappoint these theorists because it doesn't seem to demonstrate even the tiniest shred of evidence that might confirm a link between the poet and the revolutionary. Still, this does not detract from the tranquil strength of his poetry in the slightest. I am honoured to have been able to help bring this collection to life and to be able to keep the memories of the unique experience in my heart and mind. In the end, I believe that I am, like my peers, another tiny but joyful link in the long and vast chains of humanity, a person who was raised and loved by predecessors to raise and love others, to create the new exactly in the way this collection was created in the past and re-created today by our small and dedicated team of good friends. To quote Jared's tribute to his ancestors, which I would like to join in with all of you, "I am a singing, beaming arrow that your strength / shot out into infinities of hope".

Annique Estelle Arhangelskaya-Ing
4258.02.31
Auckland, ANZ North Island, Earth

Seven, or Eight Muses

The Eyes That Hold the Gentle Books

The muse, she giveth,
and she taketh away.

And the poet (if it be a man),
he stands in the shadow
of the letters her radiance
evokes in his mind.

He has been and will always remain
the circuit of passivity,
the channel in networks, a tool of the comm,
an instrument of the divine.

For without the impulse and the explosions
on the pico-scale of the brain
induced by her very hand of existence,
he ceases to be.

She plays the mother
unconsciously, aflame and often unknowing,
of a million children swimming through abstracts of the unborn,

their laughter echoing round in vast spaces
across membranes of the metaverse,
so many matrices and vectors
truly open now.

The incombustible igniting, her hands
deal in the offspring of knowledge,
the infants of the days to come,
threading trajectories of the particles

that emerge from events of horizons
into the weave of the future uncertain.

Her eyes and her hands move
with a firm, gentle sweetness
across the covers of the hereafter,
constructing the birth of a sun.

She cares probably nothing at all
of the books that she deals in;
but without the hands that touch, and the eyes that hold
the poet cannot even begin.

In the Dark We Trust

to guide our way
to find the opposite of our say
to define our light
to maintain all of our fights

in the dark we trust

here, today
be welcome, please stay
we need you the most
your cost
is the best thing to pay for

your favourite trampoline:
twelve-way sacred-street:
isolated polarities:

because it's a world coming down
and a place circling around
and around
and around,
all around

and in the darkness we trust

in the ultimate bleakness of your intention
perseverance without intervention

CCEEMPTTU Acronymics

I

people unseen
openly
encircling
territories undreamed
roving
yielding

II

yes, we should say, give us more of the same, hold our diamond
reins tighter, blindfold us thrice,
tie our night-gowns, shut our eyes, tuck in our hands and feet
                                                    (an'maybetie'em),
eloquent your good-night song;
order some more of those blisteringly colourful and brilliant
posters hanging from the walls – the Walls – the wall.

III

Players, when they get tired of the game
oh so popular today, require a challenge, an
exit, but are always given shouts and whips
to contain them on track. "Fools! Come on!",
raging they cry, "Bring those whips and chains!
Yes, you – bring them on!"

There Is No You

There is no you
there is no me
there is no I or we

just dynamic,
changing,
ever-evolving
complex signatures of energy.

So when you want to speak
your troubles in the lonely night
go back to this here thought:

there can be no you
there can be no me;

in any and all places
there are no barriers
that can halt the you with the me,
sailing together as one in the sea.

No you, no me,
no I – nor we,

just dynamic,
changing,
ever-evolving
complex signatures of energy.

Jewel-Black Beauty

A jewel in the sun,
shining with black light,

taking all the glimpses in,
soothes the broken nerve.

It's a moment of clarity
even Death sings about:

relieves me in a tiny second,
celebrates my senses;

and then the colour doesn't matter,
doesn't matter anymore.

Forget, forgive? No, I forgo the colours
for she leads me into her sublime.

Where Your Tracks Burn

Before my eyes, there's always a road,
walls I could never stand.

The cities – they mean nothing
when there's no one inside,

fireplaces,
houses I never remember,
in my mind I see only the sky
          (blue).

I've walked for hundreds of years
and walk I will right across the sea;

home's where they tread, your feet,
home is where your heart beats.

Wondering through labyrinths of hills,
lost in valleys, found on mountains

I cross
rivers
and lakes,
waters
and skies.

My feet carry me eternally.
My eyes have turned to arrows.
I feel your fragrance on the wind.
I slowly hear your tracks

because home is where they tread, your feet,
home is where your heart beats:

where your tracks
still burn.

Interaction Is

I

Interaction is
my satisfaction.
Through this night refraction
I see my dull reactions.

Living like night owls,
screaming damned ghouls,
there's no time to concentrate,
no strength to evaluate

the state of our sleep.
Are we walking like sheep?
Awake re-awake break
and change for no one's sake.

But if the mountain really sleeps,
do we set our phones to beep
or do we simply lay us down
and wait to sink into the ground?

II

Randomly flashing inflections
of freshly coined words;
defiantly blazing reflections
of undiscovered worlds.

A connection of the highest order,
always penultimate and within border:
in the ocean of uniformity,
You and I form the deformity.

Newly Posted

(*a response to Hone Tuwhare's "Rain"*)

(1 eye)

sunlight
I can feel you
burning holes in me,
sunlight

if I were blind,
I'd hear the pressure
of your rays
igniting the hairs

on the back
of my hands,
hiding
in the dark

(2 ayes)

Raining on me, although I'm well prepared.
Some people would take shelter
under those funny, funny small umbrellas.
I walk bare-headed, sunglasses.

If this is a hell, I would have to be –
a masochist perhaps? – a tester rather,
attempting to reach the limits of a
night-vision granted by uneasy pedigrees.

A child of the night – am I? A child
of my age more properly, a maniac sitting in,
an armchair hero, as the song would have it,

saying, singing my welcomes to the

night divine enveloping me, colossal
robe, unto its vista I pay my tributes,
re-posting my riposte today, under this
hellfire raining, unsuspecting skies—

and so I read your letter. It is dark,
again, I smile inside, lay on my bed,
slowly slide the letter-opener, hidden
the smooth nakedness of your paper,

ink aromas filling my room; you
unfold. No way to describe this.
A bolt comes from the dark starry skies,
I see the rays now, now I know,

my eyes wide open, lying in the dark,
I would never have a better way and place
to see you, to feel you, in your entire
strength, unfolding, grandeur and apocalypse.

You lake-mother, sphere of fire makes
all hells whimper and hide in their corners of shame,
but I will walk upright still, under your
steel rays – and you know, I realise

I like a challenge.
Hiding now, in my bedroom, wrapped
in cool sheets, I am ready
for your multiverse of shining flames.

(3 Is)

moonshine
you reflected hellfire
hello, my old friend

together

we have talked
through timeless nights
and if I were deaf,
I'd still hear your tides

in my heart and bones
(the brighter you shine,
the darker it is)
I would vanish one day

with you, moon
I will travel
into this endless
blue space

Like Interlocking Hands

Just for this single hour,
ditch the words, look at the stars, and know that they will stay,
put language to rest; and for a minute,
speak to me with fingers.

When the smoke's just cleared
– the smoke from all the battles of the day –
– the smoke you've grown with sweat these days –
you'll see the music.

The real music plays
always in the other room, and though the door is open,
it lingers at the edge of your ability to hear;
you stumble and you fear.

See how living skin inhabits
the vanishing and outer limits, the perimeters
of you that touch the future, still incoming,
the boundary of contact, lip to lip.

These rims are wheeling,
gathering momentum from the synthesis of us,
clicking in like cog-wheels of a slowly synchronising breathing,
giving strength like hands that interlock.

Reach out with cold and freezing fingers,
trace the mesh of being that we summon.
And when the fogs of noise lift up and clear,
you'll know, you'll feel: I'm here.

Flesh You Cannot Escape

You Won't

take me shake me
scrutinise me ridicule me
fake me break me
use me then abuse me

I will swallow the stone
(so sharp its edges)
I will carry all your stones
(so overwhelming their weight)

shelve me label me
disable and enable me
twist me turn me
ignite me and then burn me
to ashes

I will take in the thorn
(so sharp its tip)
I will take in all your storms
(so overwhelming the pain)

and you won't know me yet
because I am the perfect tool
purposes I have countless
suck up my endless gene-pool

throw me blow me
blame me and scold me
empty me fill me
thrill and then
kill me

The Diesel Kids

diesel power
in our veins
driving us
utterly insane

drive, drive on
uncivilised
disorganise
and utilise

and all is finished
and all is not
wake up man
say it's on

don't leave us
don't stop the song
don't chase the clouds
please love on

Killed Him

This crucible of torture can't just be explained away.

Machines are grating in my brain
that have been fed corrosive slag today.
In muzzled vision, I know of the facts,
of treachery, hypocrisy, and death:
with dying eyes, I watch him close in,
at every touch of his I scream in vacuum,
with every thrust I know it's all pretence,
and with the final push and shove I retch.
This hurt is like a sharpened axe
that the butcher drags with force
across the heaving sinews in their terror,
splitting muscle from the muscle, letting
blood clog nerves chain-sawed like violins.
My brain is tugged into dimensions
where greasy, spotty, jagged horrors dwell,
but dares not speak: it cannot harm your soul.
I know the lies in greed and flesh,
but my vision is impossible to heal.
And if you listen close, you'll hear a sound,
a sound that's made by spinal cords
torn out of brains and flesh, and broken;
I crush and grind my teeth in speechless agony,
a putrid swamp of pain, as planet-wide and heavy
as an ocean murdered thoroughly, efficiently, so long ago.
Through grinding enamel I weep,
but quietly. I will not wake my mother,
not here and not now, I will not share
this horizon, endless, burning at a million degrees.

Instead, I dry my tears in silence, clench fists
and straighten up, adjust my jacket to conceal
the weight, put my shoes on and go out.

A Mystery Link

Mystery comes in,
coughs and sniffs a bit.
Mystery sneaks in,
a breeze in her violent hair.

Mystery goes out,
notebook in bag,
Mystery goes
(does not look back)
away.

And in between
it's oh so damned noisy
but of the noise I hear nothing,
only catch a silent breathing,

the thumping of a heart,
thoughts that course through a sophisticated network,
the rhythm of a sole being
(because in this there is
        only one being).

Amidst the barriers,
I ponder.
The freeman wind whispers
in and out the safety constructions of this place.
Steve the devil sings about the firewall,
but here and today, it's no more than a tiny tiny piece
in a steel-web of neutrons

no communication seems to get through:
no wave, no electron, no postal or protocol package.
But still
there's a link underneath,
an unseeable line existing where it should not

and that weird transfer
        is burning the connection,
the uncountable bits flow
within gleaming metal.

Sparks
like larks.

It's quite impossible to paint;
the painter lets her brushes rest
while the drawing on the ground lies vague
but visible from outer space,

visible to eyes that wait,
visible to minds that listen on this wavelength,
flames visible beneath a web of living defences
who were meant to be invisible.

So Mystery walks in again
and then out
where
in between
I am in there to catch the vibrations.

So repeat, repeat!
Please repeat it:
we all live for this cycle,
    for its perennial
        re-iteration

and it's beautiful
and I love you
and it'll always shine.

Irresistible Drive

the drive delivers
my face shivers
your foundation quivers
then we're gone

mingle with divinity
and you reach infinity
leave aside affinity
it's time to let come

hollow revelations
lead to your salvation
abandon those
and choose liberation

the only climax of sanity
is the merging with insanity
disengage profanity
and enter the humane humanity

Always Already Insufficient

I might just as well give up.
There's nothing done or to be done
here on this Earth, in this universe,
to ever suffice: no act of building, no effort,
no sacrifice.
                      For I might work night-shifts
in that cold of winter darkness I cannot forget
for the freeze has seeped to the broken marrow
and taken over the creation of cells.

Or I might take up a machete, move to plantations,
reap sugar cane in the sweat of midday,
break my back on the fields of the killed,
still get my soul whipped for not caring enough.

I might spend years in shafts, digging
for the golds of the new info-age,
lithium and asbestos filling my lungs,
explosions gone wrong, trapped under rock,
and after months in the dark of Earth's skin
get nothing but scorn and derision and spit.

I might as well spend my time waiting,
killing the seconds, wishing them all now away
until you decide to make up your mind
on how to use me and my time, today and tomorrow.

But you're unsatisfied and complaining,
nervous, desirous, rejecting, obscene.

I might step into fires, put my neck into nooses,
abandon my fortunes in schemes and delusions,
cut my limbs off to save you from death,
sell my innards to pay for the depth of your skin.

Still no powers, no money, no senses,
no visions of futures and body of warmth
might ever get near to stilling your hunger.
Desires for more that rot and mortify spirits
cannot be stopped or moved off their courses.
So go forth and make more of the paper
that fills up your eyes and your lungs,
more of this viscous control that slides through your veins.

Go. Get away! Get the hell out of my sight!

Do not return to the sweating and breathing
piece of bloody machinery that is me,
this insufficient soul, failing, that thrashes in agony
for it craves the light of another.

So take up your hunger – and go!

Spilt for the Children

You and us, we ride a carousel of gigantic proportions:
spinning ever faster, our total mass accelerating,
until we get ejected on trajectories of half-lives, here.

Silent and sullen, unknowing, we carry along
the stories you gave us all, through the years.
Grandfathers and mothers, fighters for freedom,
people frightened and scared and heavy with burdens,
overloaded with work and finding no outs,
vacuumed in by histories swirling and sweeping.

No one asked them if they would like the ride.
No one asked you to give us your time.
But you did with a passion, and never thought back.
You tied the Cosmos to the donkey's tail
and slapped its back – another ride to entertain us
and teach us something useful (maybe).

So we went. Looked back from time to time
to see if you were feeling fine, exhausted still
from struggles you were pulled in without warning.
We went. And what remained for you
were empty days, the void of useless, violent news,
the Earth around the Sun, and you a passenger.

Snow grows, recedes again, then grasses, trees,
and birds return to fill up some part of the time
you wait for us. And out here, wandering amazed,
we battle abstract algebras of nonsense, minds
swollen by those things some people do for coins,
but reach out still, touching stars afar.

Oh, how we wanted you to one day come along,
board the machines you thought went to space,
join us on our trip to a galaxy of weird freedom,

marvel in awe on a different ride. But instead you got
those little bitter pills, and now you have to hunt them
at the table so that your heart won't turn belly up.

We were late. One quiet morning, the luminous Sun turned
invisible to you.
　　Today, I stand here boiling, seething,
my hands in fists, and listen to care-free stories of fun.

So hear me now: I promise you this.
You gave the blood of your time for me.
One day I'll give mine to the children.

Insufficient Science

Calling God Tonight Blues

I pick up the phone and I dial God.
The phone rings, then puts me in waiting mode.
An angelic voice tells me to stand by,
I wait, but tears well up in my eyes.

The muzak goes on, God's not online;
he's clearly busy, I'm not on his mind.
If I'm to talk to God, I'll need a flat rate,
the muzak's enough to empty my plate.

Someone picks up, I say, "Dear God, finally!"
"Archangel Gabriel here," the boom startles me,
I pull the receiver away, stare in disbelief,
hang up, then think: that conversation was brief.

Dial again, muzak goes on, God ain't online –
he's surely busy, I'm not on his mind.
If I'm to talk to God, I'll need a flat rate
the muzak's enough to empty my plate.

Catch and Hide

point the broken side up
open up the gate
the mirrors are touching the sides
the roofs are stroking the sky

these sides are running low on tears
clouds are chasing each other
in the old mazes
    of the skies' silky waters

run
or cry
play
never die

chase me, catch me and embrace me
the gardens of sorrow are closed
turn all fires on
warm yourself in them

hide yourself in me
just as I
hide
in you

CyclopSun

Blood is now oozing painstakingly
from this mind once so healthy and strong.

In waves of darkness, the bleakness of the day:
the bright eye of the CyclopSun,

watching everyone,
sub-kelvin gaze.

•

Revelation Liberation

Throw the stone into the lake
and watch the patterns, beautiful, emerge.
Throw the stone into the swamp
and get ready to be splashed with mud.

Draw the sword, then die by it,
open the gates of hell and watch the hordes swallow you;
jumping from worse to the worst,
raise a bloody hand and die first.

Tired of violence,
tired of bloodshed,
tired of the insanities
that turn the world

into senseless lead.

Look at both sides of the coin and you'll see them both:
the one wielding a quill, the other – pointing fingers.
We have to play this game: it's show *and* tell – because
we have to avoid yet another whitewashed hell

and because, in the beginning and the end,
black
is the main cosmic colour.

Crisp Waters

Crisp waters, cold, awaking.
Ghosts of cats impassively walk by,
jump over each other, shaking
the foundations of my eyes.

Surrounded by unknown trees.
Primordial – so ancient are they,
much older than the breeze,
than the soil – and these bright rays.

But I am growing down
into the wintry ground,
extending downward, stretching,
twisting further, burrowing, fetching

lethargy,
coiling
into deep
cryosleep.

So when there is
no love from family
no love from friends
no love from love

where will you search for peace?
Where will you cry at night?
Where will you warm your feet?

In silent skies above…
In silent skies above.

Upwards, soil to sky,
a desperate blow, a desperate flight
to escape the oily undergrounds,

to float in those crisp waters,
    no longer, no longer bound,

to be one with all the drowsy ghosts,
the patient ones, the furious hosts,
to stop the pain down there at the spleen,
to learn and grow with trees unseen –
        Magnificent.

Evening at the Ground Table

If time could be cut up
into slices of eternal white bread,
if it could be replayed like a record,
re-spin of black vinyl,

if it could be re-read and reformed into books,
tomes yellowish-brown that hold
      the pulse of days long forgotten,

I would keep that evening
until my swollen brains stop their tic-tac-
toeing through the endless domes
            of wild rhizomes.

My elbows on a grand table of wood,
uncounted hours of talk and sweet laugh
and the fleeting something in the air,
the human voice of your atmosphere.

The only thing I can see,
            the only thing I can speak:
you live within an ancient tree,

a home of volume against flatness; green arteries
      felt and invisible branches in reeling
where the ants carry your trains of thought

tiny shiny tireless workers,
building and re-building to the rhizomatic blueprint,
the yocto-level
of a myriad metaverses diverging and converging

in a house of warm firelight,
a place of heart and mind,
a home of home.

Inside Looking Out

Inside looking out.
Is it better now?
Still feeling betrayed?
When the masks rotate,

when you see them swap,
do you feel less left?
The watch and the abandon:
less random what you need;

but, jumping right into your face,
the action's sliding out of grasp;
the more control – more vectors;
collisions imminent, grip: off.

Infection guaranteed, virus vs. order;
watchtowers now crumble and blur.
You begin to craft a new mask
out of shimmering entropy.

Conducting Veins

I

de-elevation, de-elevation
no sleep, no sleep
keeping clocks and singing phones,
time slips,
a rug running away
    from under your feet
as it all gathers
    fills up
sticks to our sides

sucking time like a funnel
like your favourite clouds
    spoiling your weather
a resonance between earth and sky
a heart like a ball
    jumping to and fro
in *perpetuum-mobile* style

will it be eternal this time?

I can feel my hands
        changing colour
going grey
going limp
refrains from trees
        and bushes and grass
    (buttheresnomoreflowersyouknow) –
keep on turning, dear windmills
and damn, this is a road story
so I should be repeating,
        perhaps,
"no way to happiness;
    happiness lies in the way"

II

but the sun is too bright again
    it irritates my eye, my eye, my eye
        and my eye

I tend to lose it, do I not
longing for a harder pillow
when all you always crave
    is inevitably soft
        and even pink
           in softness

so why
when it's all about losing time,
    the loss should be mine
and I don't understand
why must I be so evil
(surely part and parcel of my name)
as to eat my own fourth dimension,
    fried
chronotemporal autoconsumption, a type of
        autocannibalism
remember to please wash
    the dishes
- and especially the cutlery -
when I close the eatery

a time (ugh, that word again)
to take up some bravery
probably a space to
kick this weird devilry?

the forwards-space
all the "competitors" again
a new shade ahead

of time unfamiliar
    in this brave new shadow
rooftops, treetops,
the top of all ice-cream
everybody go, run for the top!
while sitting in the middle shade;

I decide to get rained on and soaked,
the push and the shove into one,
grind me some teeth...

III

the strength immeasurable
of all the forefathers,
the musics and the people
    of the word and the sound,
and the freedom gift of
    softwares,
the surprise of beauty,
the solid light and solid air
and everything else that evades naming
another this
another that
another all:
channel
channel
channel

the conductor
alight with the energy coursing

...have to pull a bit harder on the reins,
have to decrease the pressure on my arteries and veins

Your Shabby Angel

Can you not see this?

You, the slick devil,
and me – your shabby angel.
In this combination of us,
we could explore
mountains and ocean floors
remake planets
visit the hearts of the stars
put the accent on space
          in the end.

Do you truly not find this ascending?

The Fastest Ever

You say you know the fastest thing.
You pull textbooks and say it's light,
in vacuum. But I know you know better.
You will just never admit it.

Let me put it plainly: you're wrong.
The fastest thing is way, way faster,
much quicker than the snail-mail light
in these turbid four dimensions.

And it's quicker than your freaking lasers,
it's quicker than your racing cars,
it's quicker than magnetic trains,
it's quicker than your racing aeroplanes,
it's quicker than your racing spaceships
from Sol-Z or Vestal Universal,
it's surely quicker than your Thrushgreys,
and it's always quicker than your armies.

It brings your counterparts to life
despite all distance and hindrance.
It creates identical beings in your brain
when they're not by your side in the flesh.
The fastest thing is teleportation, creation
and duplication instead of destruction.
It carries more into this universe every second
the light passes its tiny 300 000 k.

Because it's faster than your death-rays,
faster than your death-stars and pain,
faster than mass drivers from hell,
faster than your proton cannons,
faster than your antimatter mines,
faster than your nuclear missiles,
faster than your forges of hell as they suck away

star matter to bring darkness and death,
and faster than all the black holes
you may ever imagine.

You are unsure, hesitating, so
here's a rhyme to attempt persuasion:

I see you still don't believe what I tell.
You know, I begin to worry – do you feel well?
Hm, was that the tree over there off which you recently fell?
Listen closely: the fastest ever:
    E, V, O, four letters, and the first one is L.

Crossing the Wall

*In loving memory of I.
Your youthful tranquillity and quiet wisdom
live on in my heart,
and I am forever indebted
for the spark you gave to me.*

Part I: I Hope You Can

Skin
it evaporates with power
	through my skin

I am turning into
a volcanic
landscape

(others let it reside
	in their brain
or their
	muscle of blood)

because I need to
	link with you

expose and give away
	this story

discharge it, set it free
	and let it speak

although you are
	behind

this great wall

this behemoth
	of osmium galaxies

this
nuclear wall

I hope you can hear

I hope you can still
    hear me

Part II: Engineering the Game

If I am to play this game,
    I should choose a starting square.
There must be
        no electronic help,
no print, no word of mouth or foot,
just plain redemption of desire
    dropped somewhere along the way.

If I am to start again,
    I'd have to pick up all my choices,
arrange them into neat chess-mate,
assign them branches, allocate them time,
design their credits, debits,
    even organise heraldic branding.

An emblem could be, perhaps, exactly what I need.
    Remove these type-cast impositions,
let me "Create a System", renew,
replenish the battery of this ancient car,
re-enact an establishment once so firm.

As I am working on this grand design,
    eyes glued to the drawing table
following decision diagrams
planning extensions to enhance the content
of my experience always finite
sketching, piling paper in my head,
writing requirements and specifications
dumping data left right and above,
dropping memos on unsuspecting technicians,
engineering the life of a plan
    in order to live it –

somewhere down there I let – I know –
    I let your feeling
           slip away.

Part III: Confused Time, Vague Vision

Minutes are easy to count.
Hours fall into other
      statistical categorisations;
days and weeks – invisible.
Months flow in the flux of ripening rye,
      indifferent, evade the ears
of the one who listens to the steps of time.

And suddenly everything
      stares back at you for a moment,
this familiar keyboard of yours
at once seems so weird:
      the tones it produces no longer in tune
to the ticking clock within you.

Even this potato you eat
so sweet in the oven and salty
ignores the pleadings of your brain, tastes
                  faulty.

Your vocabulary appears too limited,
does no longer express your need for peace,
the sleep you expect every night.
All workload impossible,
          bureaucracy creeping,
overtired minds
          and locked up dreams.
The keys, despite the cliché,
                  have been lost
and one cannot unlock one's own toilet.

These seconds of blurred life
      do not seem like years or centuries.
These moments of vague vision
      skilfully blank one's decision.

Uncared for, time just walks away
and your stumbling thoughts
    wander out of your mouth
aimlessly, but then suddenly
    right on target
to further spread this recorded confusion.

This simple door of handshakes closes
    because you didn't prop it open.
Worst of all,
    you didn't stop for a second
        to just sit down
            and care.

Part IV: Under that Almond-tree, in Spring-time, in Blossom

When you crossed the wall,
were you met with shining colours?
Armour left to the guards outside,
did you discover your god?
Now you know:
        She's this old, old woman,
her twisting, weaving hair flowing
            with the wind,
begging for that last dime of food
you chose to withhold
        by the powers of superior discretion at your feet.

I guess you were satisfied.

But I still want to guess – your step
        the winds in your eye
the shivering feeling of air
the blood beating so much stronger than ever
        through your temples and wrists –

was there
        a minute smile on your face?
A benchmark of happiness?
            exhaustion?
            relief?
            or overcoming pain?

So, finally, when you crossed the wall,
        did you reach in the end
            the god your painting promised,
under that almond-tree,
        in spring-time, in blossom?

Part V: Search to Re-render

It's Sunday the 13th.
The moon will rise at 18:47.
Its face, full, unbending,
will watch this final TV.

Disturbing their unheeding fiesta,
she's banging away the impact of news.
Starting with a bang, going with a bang,
you could feel the pieces of the incoming
dark
– if you were there –
making reality bumpy,
the chunks warping the surfaces
of the air in between us all.

She does not respond to his
looking for her under tree and stone.
The world is slowly being re-rendered,
re-tailored to fill in the blanks,
stretched and re-drawn to colour the holes
and we all start to seem a bit unreal,
our faces elongated, expanded with
reddish complexions, and
we have actually lost this wonderful
ability to talk (but only for a while).

He contemplates flight, an unyielding process.
His search fruitless in eternity,
he sits down in front of the singing machine
and watches his fingers run.

It is Monday,
    the 14th.

Her children – unconceived, unborn – kicking

and screaming and biting and caressing,
grow in the multiple wombs nested in his cortex,
safely hidden to live on through him.

Part VI: Abacus Muted

You said nothing, so did I
we liked this shut-up state
it's so comfortable – and wild!!
I ignored the energy, you seemed to have
done so too; I missed the point
of contact, you seemed so surprised
and hurt and I repeat to myself
how could I know but I knew
all along, but was always uneasy
to wake the hungry monster let it
eat its pie and maybe relieve
someone's soul in the process get dirty
with guilt and sin and damnation
of friends' relativity public eye
and yearly devotion and remove
that stain of failure and dysfunction
a socio-emotional smart-o-pathological
refuse, to drench ourselves in this unearthly
rain

your umbrella was as colourful as mine.
This cybernetic info-flow with no physical
connection remains inexplicable to science
even today when every refrigerator
would have computed our compatibility,
my pocket PC would have called me a fool,
sang it to me as a little coffee machine ditty,
        a bloody ring-tone.

These useless laments are still
useless, the hunger continues, despite
charity, except only for your charity
but you chose to withhold it
by losing your ability to speak
and you said nothing

and so did I
    and it's gone:

this imperfect perfection
forever longed-for "it"
this unstable salvation
    uncontrollable wit.

And if I'm talking to my notebook today,
I'm perhaps in need to say sorry
but these primitive devices
    an abacus here and there
they cannot bridge the wall,
their lightning electro-organic connections
are always mute, in awe of my silence,
and I don't seem to be capable

of any imagination
to see into you and your patterns
the way you made your decision
the way you calculated hurt
and injury and insult and life
and chose to stop,
    and go in the end.

Part VII: Comprehending the Steps

Immediate hunger, undisclosed rain,
private typhoons, deniable challenges,
what we seek to quench:
the cheating veil of the future,
the faltering bank of our knowledge.
Even clocks get sometimes tired of ticking,
but never we,
the relentless, un-ground-able,
imposing our revisions every day anew,
we could not halt
to save our lives;
was it not just like that with you?
Were you not listening
    on any wavelength at all?
Not paying enough useless currency
to lease that puny, half-automatic
effort to try and make out
my voice against the shifting crowds?

For I needed my words to arrive at your doors
and I loved the flowers in your window,
all the blue yellow green red.

Why couldn't we downgrade the stampede,
restrain that rush,
undo what had been undoable still?
I wish we all could
lay down, arrange the pillows cosily,
light up our pipes,
inhale that vanilla tobacco
once per day – once per week –
once per month, damn it!
Forget for a moment the computing of units
ride on the flux
re-adjust to that pendulum-born oblivion

sink in and soak through
let alternating currents surround us:
conscious, unconscious,
              conscious-unconscious,
re-link hibernation and dreaming and brain.

And I can now only hope
that you are listening
and perhaps have a vague idea
of all the crazy things that I mean to say.
I was tagged mad and insane, yet despite this
I somehow am sure
you watch me
but no longer wait.
I know you're in motion,
I see you, the archer
              and her many arrows
flying towards apples and pears and peaches,
their juice trickling, running down your chin
across your heaving heart,
filling the well of your navel...

I feel the grass underneath your back,
your cats playing or lying around you,
the sun shining, the rain of spring falling
– the devil's wedding proceeding
      with full fanfare, greeting you welcome.
Your journey has finished.
The devil, that old entertainer:
just the first of your guests.
An eternal list of visitors
a new existence
a new insistence on the never-end
a new journey into forever.

Somehow I'm sure of your crossing.
You have reached through.
You have travelled across.

I see you now
behind the wall
behind the great concrete steel diamond constructions
in dimensions too many to count,
behind the mammoth iridium nuclear wall
in the gardens,
    resplendent,
        beyond.

"Too Much Love"

Another One for the Purple (Colour of Your Eyes)

The colour of your eyes
seems to remain within
although the lights are gone
and the walls are getting thin.

Without you there can be no life;
music silent, lamps outside,
shadows never will be ripe.
Dark surrenders to the neon lights
       of the streets
       through the sheets
       with the beatings
       of the greed.

But mirrors will reflect nothing,
electricity will run through circuits;
through pipes, water will be hopping
and the fridge won't want to quit

until the colour of your eyes
roams again into the drawers' secrets,
then chases out them all the flies;
then follows pathways of the jets,
       through silent skies –

'cos it erases all the echoes of my cries
heard over towns and across the districts
and brings back here all sweet sighs,
re-igniting life and instincts.

Sentenced to Distances

this enormity
of insipid conformity
thoughts interconnected
minds thoroughly over-reflected

(and as I watch,
    she grows into a tree)

spirits neglected
loves rejected
this momentary affection
overrules the inflection
    of I

(and as I silently
    comprehend,
        she grows free)

sentenced to distances
we never really touch the bottom
sentenced to approximate
we cannot find the unity
        (within her and the tree)

the table never ends
but you keep pulling it your way
the tale forever bends
but you still believe in hearsay

the warmth of the old man's lamp
        will comfort you
as he keeps on ever searching
for the human being, already gone

and I'll still be seeing your face

imagining the parallel reality
our divinely beautiful mortality,
our secret triumph looming
(large on the horizon of events)

Longing (Nothing's Over)

I am lying in the dark before the dawn
and waiting for you to be reborn.

I am in the end (just the man afraid)
of the same darkness deep within

and I'm fighting it
pushing

and bleeding again
from where I breathe.

I coagulate
and the clots
grow to a crust that keeps me from air.

Without your vehicle,
I await the blindest of dooms.
Please
don't leave me longing
for the scent of blue skies.

For I,
I want to hear a voice
that belongs to you,

I want to see the light
of your moving hands
against the grey sky,

I want to watch the sparks
in the stormy fathoms of your eyes
bring on the dawn.

I want to be

yours

in every universe
on every path of time
with every beat of the sentient mind.

First Binding

There is no comprehending this:
no logical instruction, no schematic bliss.
In through the desert of the grinding stones,
souls stumbled blindly, met; sparks shone.

And distances don't matter when the current's running,
and wear and tear don't show after the second coming.

So I speak those words which maybe matter not to you.
I bind myself: I'll see the binding through.

Through death and sorrow and the pain
of suffering and cold pecuniary gains,
through exhaustion bordering on twisting fever,
through the illness of eternal shivers,
through the lies of petty hypocrites and cheaters.

The binding burns our throats like those of youngest fire-eaters.

And though the binding is imbalanced; though
its fire is as freezing as the deepest winter's snow,
I plant it ever deeper into this Earth's crust;
for all else here is vacuum, desert,
        and howling nuclear dust.

Love and the Cold

I love the cold.
I love the forces of the rain,
the tiny warriors storming bravely
the dryness of your skin.
Click and clack, down-pouring
    softness on my back.

Sometimes
    a more severe cold
wills a hail to life
    (you run and hide),
but my love stays wild
    as the stones of ice rain down on us
like dimes of the believers
down a spacious wishing well
    in the village of your mother tongue.

Stones in a well devoid of echo
    keep the coolness of the living water
that nourishes the shade
    of every silent tree
your parents and grandparents sowed.

I bask beneath the shadow
of every cloud that brings me shelter
from the scorching anger of the Sun.
You stand, a silhouette of warmth
against the damping, looming
    shadows of the Sun.

The Confession and the Explanation

Last night I dreamt of a poem,
a confession that would tell you
everything I ever wanted said
about you, and me, and the bonds –
luminous, ascending force fields –
that spread and hold between us.

But then – was it a garbage truck?
my noisy, thoughtless neighbours?
some row exploding on the street?
I was awoken, and the poem left.
In vain I looked for it in music,
in works of literature and film,
in silences of forests and the clamour
of the spaceports and the main streets.

And long I cried and circled in despair,
and sought replacements in the air.

So after days of turmoil, pain,
I sat exhausted in the darkness
of one night, and watched the stars.
They spoke to me, the madman.
Told me this elaboration I was seeking
is too precise, too strangling,
too tight for motion's beauty.

I saw I'd been a fool. For what design
might ever hope to clarify
the gorgeous and unearthly
in these synchronicities of quanta
that bring your hands to mine?
Whose drawers full of definitions,
whose bulky wardrobes full of classes,
divisions, categories, forms,

might ever dream of sorting
the chaos of the life that we create?

And I was sad that I would have
to come to you again empty-handed.
Goodness, was I sad...but then
I felt the weight of something old
I've always carried with me,
an abstract load of rusty speech.
Those were three words, so
tattered, overused, but shining
now, in the deepness of the night.

And this is what I bring to you today:
three words so plain, so broken,
abused and tortured and so drained,
worn out, dumped, and then forgotten,
a cliché from the dawning of time.

Still they glow in the bleakness
and lead me to you, radiate the light
that makes time stop and run.
And I would say them to you, but...you,
my starlight, already know them well.

Egotistical Paramour Comparativism

You're not good enough.

You're not smart enough.
You're not fast enough.
You're not diligent enough.
You're not efficient enough.
You're not hard-working enough.
You're not funny enough.
You're not brilliant enough.
You're not entertaining enough.
You're not slow enough.
You're not patient enough.
You're not competitive enough, and you're not cooperative
                                                    enough.
You're not silly enough.
You're not silent enough.
You're not planning ahead enough.
You're not playful enough.
You're not tranquil enough.
You're not surprising enough.
You're not dangerous enough.
You're not wild enough.
You're not cute enough.
You're not scientific enough.
You're not explosive and loud enough.
You're not creative enough, and you're not destructive enough.

You're not complex enough.

You're not pompous enough.
You're not pretentious enough.
You're not shallow enough.
You're not vain enough.
You're not ludicrous enough.
You're not capricious enough.

You're not academic or abstract enough.
You're not marketing enough.
You're not addicted enough, and you're certainly not addictive enough.
You're not self-centred and self-obsessed enough.
You're not dumb and stupid enough.
You're not ignorant enough.
You're not unreliable enough.
You're not blindly religious enough.
You're not superstitious enough.
You're not cheating or deceptive or fraudulent enough.
You're not hypocritical enough.
You're not ultra-nationalist enough.
You're not scary enough.
You're not aggressive enough.
You're not fascist enough.
You're not capitalist plus neo-liberal enough.
You're not violent enough.
You're not murderous enough.
You're not profitable enough.
You're not manipulative enough.
You're not treacherous enough.
You're not dishonourable enough.

And you're also not broken enough, inside.
You're not twisted enough.
You're not exhausted enough.
You're not empty enough.
You're not sleepless enough.
You're not troubled by your past enough.
You're not losing it enough.
You're not tearful and randomly crying enough.
You're not tortured and tormented enough.
You're not pulverised by pain enough.
You're not delusional enough.
You're not insane enough.
You're not bipolar enough.
You're not paranoid enough.

You're not depersonalised enough.
You're not psychotic enough.
You're not schizophrenic enough.
You're not deliberately self-harming enough.
You're not suicidal enough.
You're not deconstructive enough.
You're not atomised by agony enough.
You're not technologically mutilated enough.
You're not remotely controlled enough.
You're not mass-equivalent enough.
You're not corpuscular enough.
You're not quantified enough.
You're not molecular enough.
You're not nuclear enough.
You're not frozen enough.
You're not metallic enough.
You're not electrified and energised enough.
You're not irradiated, not anywhere near enough.

You're not radiant enough.

And you're simply not evil enough.

For me.
For me.
For me.

Not yet.

The Shivers

There's a new disease in town,
and the citizens are running from it.
Fear spreads like the fog in the morning
between houses and palaces, gardens and shops.
The shivers they call it, and flee.
The victims are dying for days now,
no end to dreadful trembles in their hearts.
No governments, no empires know of any cure.

Today…today we learn the morbid news:
you and me, we quiver, we have been infected.
Contagious we are as the soon-to-be-dead;
some shun us; some curse us; some implore us to leave.
So we move to the outskirts, the skin
of the city, the apple orchards we enter in bloom,
your grandfather's old cottage in walnut-tree shadows,
and there await the truth of our death.

Days go by with the shivers. We shudder
and shudder with every beat of our hearts.
Slowly we learn the harmony of our breathing,
sharing a bed, a table, a floor and a mind.

Seven days – and an eighth night comes.
We sit under moonlight in summer, and tremble
like the aspen trees in the absence of wind.
Then you move closer and do the surreal:
Your fingers touch mine and I quiver.
Your knees touch mine and I shudder.
Your eyes touch mine and I tremble.
Your heartbeat joins mine and we shiver.
We shake the trees, the skies, and the waters.
Our tremors are locked into waves of the light.
And we shiver away the pieces of time lost.
We shed all the loss and are made whole again.

Cured, we go hand in hand back to the city.
People are speechless, their mouths open wide.
I look deep inside you and find you determined.
Our time is at hand, we will go and spread far
the word of our cure, of the unison lived.
You look back into me and hold my hand fast,
and I know what you feel: in my soul
remain only your eyes and your smile.

Vanilla Democracy

Sherbet, frozen, on a stick,
champagne in your marzipan,
stracciatella over ice
with almonds or with walnuts
or with both plus lemon cream,
but still I ask for vanilla.

Cherries, strawberries
and mangoes on your hands;
curry chocolate coating
grating at your teeth;
sugars in brown flames:
I decline, and call for vanilla.

Coconuts exploding
in the milkshake seas of grape;
brandy liquors burning
in the fruity yoghurt of the night;
caviar volcanoes –
still I caress and kiss vanilla.

One Condition Away

Heaven is always one condition away.

The road sign: that arrow just beyond the reach
of your tired, dry, myopic eyes.
The building block: the screw that twists and turns
and mocks you, but will no longer fit.
The tool of work: an old, unsteady hand
that refuses to cooperate with the future of the tech.
And love: the lips that someone else
caresses now, pale with the distance of the loss.

If you could touch the arrows with your gaze,
gather and arrange the elements in breathing function patterns,
steel the aim of those arthritic, gentle fingers
and hold the hand of love again between your palms,

would not heaven be attained, forever?

Heaven is always one condition away.

But you will do well to remember (for the future holds pain):
if the link once existed – though now severed –
the memory of it means heaven is forever attained.

The Four Siblings

The University of Anger

Sweet, and holy anger.

The seeds are inside you:
the pain of harness on your neck
the laughter from the haves
the twists and jokes of the secure
the moaning of the artificial art
the dreams of zombies from the safe
the schemes of Profet from the slayers.

Hold the seeds, don't let them go;
nurture them with dull pain from your back;
leave their roots to mingle
    with the cramps in legs of overwork;
and pour inside the holy water of the eyes.

Trees now growing in the garden,
till the soil of yesterdays,
    remove the weeds of slumber pacified.
Sit down and meditate in gardens of the dead:
the trees of anger grow,
    and their fruit electric ripens.
Hold
this invigorating juice,
    this energy of many dead in pain;
ferment, foment, and seethe in frying power.

Critical mass obeys the law of the living.
The higher you get, the harder you fall –
that is, the agony which they inflict
returns to take their entities in tolls
of sleepless years, unbroken tinnitus
       and loss,
heart-cancer, infirmity of the mind,
    control now gone, the vast empires empty.

So hold the liquid of the anger,
    let it grow in oils of blood and sweat.
Eat of the fruit electric,
    summon up the muses of the lost:
the thin, the fat, the ugly and the fair,
the dark, the black, albinos, pure air,
the twisted, the righteous, the short and the tall,
the muttering, the haughty, the ones of the fall.
And listen closely, listen:
    a myriad muses sing into my ears:

Oh sweet, and holy anger!

When you hear those discordant voices,
release the furies, let them pour like lightning:
out onto the slayers of the weak
out onto the robbers of the fallen
out onto the killers and their Profet
out onto the rapists of the silent and the small.

Then let me build this school of anger:
I'll teach the little ones to know,
to grow the trees of yesterday,
to learn of peace, and grass, and snow.
Someday it will be their turn to build it all:
the trains, the planes, the ships and cars,
the hospitals, the roads, the houses and the schools,
the factories, the labs, the libraries, the bridges,
and the vehicles that one day, every day,
        will take them to the stars.

But if the sweet and holy anger
is overcome with filth
of murderers and rapists,
of those who rob the weak and small:
sit back there, in the garden;
meditate upon the blessed dead;

and summon up the anger's siblings:
    the rage, the fury, and the love.

For a Piece of Contact

and when they tell you
in words bright, glowing
of the new orders
        and when they show you
        in pictures shining, hyper-elemental
        their brave worlds
   and when they have you
   eat the final mint
   so that your brain explodes
      "don't, don't believe what you read"
      and maybe – maybe you'll be freed
      from the reins
        with the rain-doors above
        open again to immerse us all
        there's a contract failing
        to leave behind
so we prepare for the drought
sell a kidney for a piece of contact
get used to the sun scorching
recycle some nuclear waste to eat

     but
     tell me, will I probably dream
     just from time to time
     of the days when there was rain
     of the nights
        we could sing in choirs
        we could connect through the net
        we could play without regret
        we could still be children

  wait for the time   these words will be smudged
when all of their stories   when the rain falls on them
  will be just talking   your pain shall be judged
    in a lack of words   by a way of a zen

so they make us
to remain apart
but we strike back
with the beat of heart

          I stand   You stand
He   She   They
   stand

but
We stand
in the end.

Cut Your Voice

Overload and bed-ache
witches dance abroad
red and orange
the colour of the Earth
a place you'd like
    to sink into
        to rest?

The pressure in your ears
seeps through your fingertips
don't go, don't leave the fear
don't give up looking just yet.

An annoying voice that blabbers on
destroys the bushes' shade,
that warm and funny feeling
dissipated by a voice so fake.

And the more you're feeling sleepy,
idea bluish in a cheekbone,
fan-like tail is seen for miles,
a burning sign that shows a tree...

So they cut your voice
because you always talk
way way *way* too much
and then, the story's over.

Reemuv-Lha's New Vampires

We come at night or at day
eyes into which a static permanent
    redness is slowly creeping
we take up your space
we eat up your food
we also of course waste your time
       so precious
we close your doors
and clean your rooms
we dust your floors and eat the dust
we trouble your sleep and provide chaos
we slow down your world-wide economy
cause a crisis or two, three when convenient
re-invent crime five times per day at the least
certainly are responsible
    for epidemic endemic developments.

We come from the east and the south
from lands of unseen mountains and valleys,
also surprisingly rivers and fields, lakes
       and forests,
and even more shockingly surprisingly:
parliaments, presidents, governments, electricity
roads and toilets and planes and the net.

But if you take the world map and turn it
upside down, head over heels
east becomes west, south becomes north
so it no longer matters
    (at least never mattered to you)
what I've been babbling about
because
we come from the east and the south, from lands where
the sun also sets and there is night
and we come out at every inverted dawn

to suck out the blood of your life, and more.

So now you know the answer:
        yes they say we're open,
our mouths are wide open to swallow you whole.

We are a new type of vampire,
and your blood's way too thin
to quell our appetite, our tall hunger.
We shall devour your intestines, your hearts
and your brains, yet before that we shall
rape your men, children, and women,
        whichever whenever applicable,
torture and murder and play with our food,
we shall extract all your juices, prepare
to boil you, to roast you, to sauté
    and to can you.
And then, with the cans, we shall go home
          and show
our families all of the pictures.

We shall do all of that, yes.
And more, so much more.
For we are the new vampires. Remember this
and never forget: because *you* invented it.

The Devil Works

The devil works alone
with a heart of bone.
The devil works at night;
no candlelight but lamps,
electric as one still may be.
Eclectic, the word, becomes dirty.

The devil rides the train backwards.
One listens for the lacking fury
of a smoking diesel engine.
Looking at the scenery in travel,
the past fields turning into a present;
that attempts to distance itself,

remains visible with binoculars.
As always, the devil don't sleep:
part of a self-imposed torture,
test the endurance of fiendish nature;
writes nonsensical villages till dawn,
chickens coo one to morning drowse.

The devil works while angels laugh.
Another afternoon spent in debate.
One knows, one is certain there is,
there was, will be, no point in
keeping up the excellent results,
but still goes on to debate anyway.

The devil toils beneath tunes
that seem to give rhythm and solace
but no one besides wants to hear.
The devil, "he smoke 'em harmonies like cigars",
relishes top-secretly, way all devils do.
Soon, the music is over, the theatre gone.

Angelic laughter fills devil's study
carrying a fleeting accusatory quality.
The devil, unhinged, looks on to see:
the well-known diaphanous angels enter.
And one is certain again, one knows for sure
that when they, at length, take those masks

off –
them angels, them grand elder fiends –
they'll be guffawing
with sadistic derision, with the scorn
of their old, well-trained harmful joy
underneath.

Breaker of Circles

You require me defined.
You're an inquisitor, a paparazzo.
You want me numbered, theorised,
you need me quartered and then drawer-ed.

So listen and I'll say this loud and clear:
I break them circles, that's just what I do,
I kick the knacks from beneath the wheels
and let the trains roll through.

Not strange that you are shocked now.
A circle's always neat and cosy.
You stagger off, will find somehow
your required daily circle doses.

But listen, listen or you'll miss it:
I break them circles, that's just what I do,
I kick the knacks from beneath the wheels
and let the trains roll through.

What Cannot Do Us in

They would've said we're efficient like wolves in a pack
efficiency seems to be to know when to defend and attack
it's high time to be already rebuilding the shack
of those who are not spoons therefore impossible to stack.

Truly to see into a person requires them, at some side, to have
been cracked
but the info that leaks make some fret, regret; even takes them
aback
so much so we have no time for that, we never cut no slack
time is brief, no need to tell me, I've read more than the F.A.Q.

What cannot do us in – you let it rain on us like wartime flak
the bombs and the noise and the shouts all to make us retract
well-prepared, you put each person a dozen knives in their
backs
and it hurts; still we'll never be the dollies on your racks.

You really do become inventive – now that you want to take us off
our track
your strategy may break – shall never bend us; and you should
know this, jack:
we don't need your hyper-philosophy tracts
we already have the grip on our facts
of life.

Gigachiroptera Sapiens Reforming

Did my red eyes betray me?
I haven't slept that much lately.
Murder and void bring it all down,
gather the fleet of insomnia.

I've been kept in this place for too long now.
My words have not really been mine.
Locked on this continent with that many rooms,
I wane and tire and bleed all around.

And did my talk go off again to reveal me?
Your impositions have made me unsafe.
A sign of disjointing, this breakage linguistic;
a vestige of falling, silence and snaps.

Strayed I have too far in this venture,
knowing not how you manage to make me
move along, play along, be along here.
Reflections of horror now finally shake me.

Liberation and peace what I fought for.
Today I am simply the next in a line,
a thoughtless device of your plan and un-plan.
This thought now leads me to rage, and abuse...

But violence is futile, a storm in a sink:
the more I vomit it, the faster you feed.
The void in the holes at the cores of your brain,
so hungry and fathomless, lives for the kill.

Conditioned or not, your control cannot stop
and obscure the rays of the sun from my gaze.
The dawn I now see after years of waiting
is cloudy and rainy, and pregnant with change.

I will open the door, jump down in the water,
glide off into sunrise with dew on my wings,
shoot out in a rocket, bring in the rain
to fill in your holes and plug you in whole.

When I smash out the window,
waters will rush in, cold and so true,
wash off your hold on me and on you.
I bring in the flood. Be ready to go.

The Censor Outside

"…scies nihil esse in istis terribile nisi ipsum timorem."
(*Lucius Annaeus Seneca*)

I am the power to stop and to clean you
to wipe the filth off your page
I am the force to say halt or continue
I am the fear that you dread.

I am the falling injunction
I am the thread cut too short
the thought of your own extinction
the place you are finally bled.

I am the one to cut you out of the black page,
            to shred and discard you,
wild music silenced inside you;
the sewer that swallows the notes.

I am the glasses that strain
and stifle the visions of flight,
the limit, the border, the wires,
the fence that deadens your gait.

I am the product of horror, a mind
gone to the verge of its own abyss,
and I tremble forever before you
knowing you'll jump off
            into bliss.

Fissure and Flux

I am nothing but a flaw
in the ten-dimensional pixel-meme matrix
of your connections to the substrates
of the universe.
I am nothing but a fault.

Not a fault-line in your brain,
not a fold of the cortex,
but a crack in that surface,
a bleeding opening into the depths.

You need me.
You need this natural incision
which leads to reservoirs
of secret toxic blood
and drains the pressure from the centres
you need so desperately to survive.

I am the flaw, I am the fault, I am the flow.

But I'm insufficient, microscopic,
a tiny tear in the edifice
that feeds your system
with rigidity and fossils.

You need a million of me.
You need a legion.
You need to purge the secret chambers
which others have installed without consent
before your birth, ahead of your conception.

I am the fissure and the flux.

I am transfiguration. I am revolution.

If This World Teaches You

If this world teaches you you're better off alone
that you need no one to talk to, confide in
that you require nothing but solitude
to move forward and bloom and endure
that the advances of isolating thought
will take you through the human swarm

and if this world teaches you gold is a standard
that accumulation overrides sharing
that wealth should be piled up inside fortresses
that your home is your lair and within
you will bask and tan yourself in gold's shine
that the coin is stronger than the hand it is in

and if this world preaches to you to walk on your own
to leave old links in the past and accelerate
to outrun everyone on your track, like a racer,
then race against friends and their fires
to stay in cold houses and not search for survivors
to wander alone the freezing highways of nuclear winter

and if this world preaches to you that numbers cannot be music
that algebra lives for cost optimisation
that reasons for action never come from philosophy
but follow the paths of "compute and eliminate"
that winners are ratios and losers are nothing
that nothing and no one are safe from the cutter

so if this world teaches and preaches all this, nothing else,
and if its teachers and preachers arrive at your home,
point guns at your head and force you to follow,
threaten your children, threaten your parents,
hold every society hostage to their ugly and broken
blood-fuelled devices, greed, folly and death,

then stand up and push back
and join hands with others
because this world is no good
and should be undone: together,
tear down death, then
build life instead.

Dear Old Bear (A Letter to a Prisoner)

Poor old bear, where are you going to?
You were sailing for freedom, but now you are through.
The storm caught up with you and sold you down creek.
The vision was broken and started to creak.

Poor old bear, with whom do you belong?
There is no one to hug you, to sing you a song.
You trotted the globe a mile at a time every day,
but the wind filled your eyes and led you astray.

Just a poor old bear with nothing to eat.
They beat you again and again till you bleed,
threaten and lie and pretend they mean good;
should have run when you knew you still could.

Dear, dear old bear, now you are blind:
they came with the scissors, stabbed you from behind.
Once your fur was a refuge, all warmth and silk,
now they left you an eye half full of milk.

Your neck has been hit and cracked at the side,
from the crevice now peeks a wild, shattered mind.
Above gather all kinds of vultures and birds,
and, dear old bear, I know that it hurts,

but though your arms have been torn, your feet still stand strong;
they may laugh at you now, but you'll charge them headlong,
and the fury and fire in the depth of your blazing white eye
will show them, dear bear, that you still know how to die.

Ivaylo R. Shmilev

116

...With the Future Always Uncertain

Monument to a Child Fast Asleep

A monument to rain and sunshine,
a monument to grass and bees,
another one to distant rays of stars,
one to a tree, another to a child.

Is this all there is out there
for me? Am I bound or shackled,
am I harnessed or restrained or
both, into a life of building

monuments, but never rain.

And tears – are they not your scientific
calculable yes
    assignable equivalent
that natural precipitation you

are always so afraid of?
My question marks ought to retreat.
Just a wheel (with teeth, my father
said), just a device, a gadget, an

appliance. And though we made them
talk, those grinding wheels never ask.
Inform and instruct, and build
monuments shall I, a blunt-toothed
wheel.

But still try
to read the dictionary,
or at least

the 2% of it
which do not watch
and count my every word.

When Solitude

When I sing myself a sobbing goodnight
in the grey of the 5 am haze
when I wake up in frequencies, go to the hundreds

when I start to blaspheme against powers of many
a card and a magic, maps and the dice
when all friendly power has the cross of the minus
when solitude overflows and tightens its grasp

when I hear my heartbeat in light-bulbs explode
when the aunts of reflection cry out for their budgets
when time's never enough for all of your objects
when my favourite father tells me that, too,
one day I would want to be rich as well

when the ceiling collapses upon all of my books
when your brain becomes obsolete to make way for your looks
when you cancel the music, shut down my PA

when I stop
    to believe in love and its devils

when the flame sighs and the impulse of black holes
pulsates incessantly in the crimson of blood.

Past the Layered Stones

I'm just another fat, foul-smelling monster sitting
on this pressure-cooker of a planet.
I've perhaps already overstayed my welcome,
overdone my public feelings, outrun all decency.

But there are four stones here, in the open,
in the flaming gardens in four corners of this place.
These stones are heavy,
forever pregnant with their pasts,
they hold me bound and captured and in silent tears.

One is Mercurial; another Martian; the third is Terran;
and the fourth, impossible, Venusian.
The layers that will always sleep within them and like arrows
point from origins into infinities of space
have come from depths uncovered by industrious
and sometimes overzealous diggers,

though that is not their miracle. The link
which holds them all together unconnected
across the vastness of a planet
lives inside the close-knit layers; deep inside the strata
shaped by violent impacts of the rocks
that carried everywhere the precious molecules of life.
Today we use these layered stones to mark the dead.

For the dead remain together
beyond the great galactic neutron walls
that encircle us, the living, divide us from the ones
we so long to embrace; deny us.
And here I remain in orbit, around around around
four stones of ancient layers
that signify primordial attachment
and speak with quiet honour: we have not forgotten.

Four stones, four different planetary cradles.
One of you flew too close to the Sun;
another was detached from time to time, but red at heart;
another was an elder mother, loving, loved, indelible, exhausted;
and yet another drew impossible trajectories
that, relentless, led to joyful futures.
I have forgotten none of this, but still
I must extend my orbit past these layered stones, away in
rhythmically growing
elliptical mechanics.

Past the old stone layers, past these layered rocks
is where I need to be, past the stones
so I can meet you once again, past the Venus Terra formed
is where I have to go, beyond to see myself more clearly
on a trajectory of mine. I'll leave the flaming gardens
of our Venus, our loving planet, to draw my ways in distant skies,
and then return one day, kneel at your layered stones
and say with honour: I am your successor,
I am a singing, beaming arrow that your strength
shot out into infinities of hope.

Those Mindless Tourists

I

I met a new ship three months ago. You know
how it works, you go online, see what your friends
are doing, get into chats with some people,
and whoop, there's a private message, hi there,
I'm a ship looking for a fun crew, I happen to know
this and this and that friend of yours, they told me
you've been shipless for a while, wanna
meet up? My old one had decided to go
on a double research mission: have a look at
a bunch of strange black holes orbiting each other
at the end of an opposite arm, and also get out of
galaxy-centre interference to better observe
several quasars. It meant it would be away for about
eight to nine years, and I could neither stop its thirst
for scientific discoveries nor go along for the ride.
So I said yes back then, and yes again three months ago.

II

This coincidence proved fruitful. Jared,
an old schoolmate of mine I hadn't heard of in years,
resurfaced with a quiet pop from the slumber of the past.
There was so much to catch up on, so the ship,
me travelling with it back home to Venus from the belt,
jumped into our talk and suggested that, instead of
spending so much time sitting in virtual rooms and
neglecting our bodies, we should pack up,
go for an excursion, a vacation to some place both
entertaining and beautiful. So we set our sights
on Awlvameerrh III (you know, the antebellum
Kepler-37i) and were on our way within the week.

Two days at a leisurely speed, and we were in
paradise. It looked like paradise from orbit,
it smelled like paradise when we got out on the ground,
it felt and tasted like paradise in the water
and in the forests. Only the noise was a bit grand,
but well, tropical climates. Awlvameerrh III was
on the languid slope of cooling off, had been
for millions of years after something unexpected
stopped, even reversed its runaway greenhouse.
What that meant for us was life. So much life
doing everything thinkable everywhere all of the time,
we were overwhelmed and chose to retreat
behind heavy hotel isolation every night, to sleep.
The days were overflowing with colour and sound,
everything basically untouched. (There had been
some colonists in the twenty-eighth and the twenty-ninth,
but they'd been just a handful of lonely and very
tired people, certainly in no shape to cause any
great damage.) The ship was immensely enjoying itself,
it went around the planet with some local guys,
biologists, mapping and counting several species
of giant flying ants and trying then to tag them
with specially miniaturised follow-up transmitters.
Most of which quite futile of course, but also very much
fun.
    Meanwhile Jared and me, we trampled
through jungles, tried and failed to climb mountains,
went underwater with subs to observe and to bask
on small, uninhabited islands, all the time talking.
The place felt so incredibly connected, integrated,
as if nothing ever cut a food-chain or severed symbiosis
violently, with purpose or without. At the time,
I was working in mineral extraction, transportation,
raw ore preparation and the like, but my university
ecology still nagged me on that planet: this was truly,
barring malevolent intervention, a planetary paradise.
For millions of Terran years to come. And all the links
seeped sluggishly by dusk and dawn into our talk.

III

I told Jared all the good tales, all the bad.
My husband leaving me, my previous job going all
haywire and mad after that, in the wake of
empty days me falling unexpectedly for a girl,
her rejection, the waves of time seemingly worthless
and I just a target pole, obsolete and abandoned.
It turned out he'd had it somewhat worse.
His girlfriend of twelve years, whom I knew as well,
broke up with him, telling him they had become deeply
incompatible, for he'd grown insufficient scientifically;
that to a man known for his creative inclinations that
had much more to do with poetry, performance, music,
theatre as well. Still he counted her as one of his muses,
one among only seven or eight in his life until then.
Too few, he complained, a true artist is always inspired
by everything, everyone, everywhere. Now that
didn't convince me, but we left the point for our
philosophical debates later on. He just said that,
like this ancient song by a rock band (I know, *rock*!)
from some time in the twentieth, "too much love
will kill you" and can do so anytime. He carried
so much heavy love inside. (And I got none, of any
given kind.) The worst news, though, was that one
of his siblings had died. An accident compounded
by previous addiction, the doctors had pronounced.
He only added that sometimes you cannot escape
the desires of your own flesh. With that I could
only agree. The brain, the exalted human brain,
it broke so frequently even today, in times of rapid
medical advance and even faster medical aid.
Without control, without the proper healing signals
the rest of human existence simply fell through.
So the least we could do four ourselves – and perhaps
for each other – is ensure we had some form

of control over ourselves so that we could stoop down,
pick up the broken pieces of minds, glue them
back together, maybe re-arrange them in a manner
that fits the newest challenges more smoothly,
fill the gaps with the ore of everyday miracles.
Because we cannot do anything for each other
as long as we are fractured, cracked, fragmented
inside. No matter what any fashion of underdone
sarcasms and deconstructions will tell you,
the living whole is much more than the sum of its
organic and mineral parts. And what better miracle
to glue you back into life than this paradise here?

IV

One tiny double incident remained in my head.
We were going to the toilet before heading back
into the jungle one morning (Jared for number one
because, he said, he was no Geschäftsführer
that day – whatever the hell that must have been;
and me to check on my absorbent since I was
having my period; yes, I'm one of the Naturals)
when Jared, not paying attention because of jabbering
on, tried crossing the wall instead of the threshold
which resulted in a silly scene from a comedy,
a blunder on a stage. Good he didn't really hurt himself.
Without a moan, he picked himself up and jested about it,
as is his custom, a thing I appreciate in a friend.

When I came out, I found him listening surreptitiously
to an old man complaining to a couple of ladies.
"Those mindless tourists," I heard the man grumble,
"they go everywhere and they all do their stuff with robots
these days. Not like when my ancestors came. We had
only ourselves to rely on, no fancy machinery. We had
to work manually, cover ourselves with calluses, battle
all the trillion revolting beasts on this insane planet. I say we

managed quite alright, although the skanky bastards
survived, way too many of them. Those foul giant flying ants?
I don't know what they call them and I don't wanna know;
I say we kill them all right now! Not study them! Not chase
them like kids, like deranged lunatics! But these tourists?
They're just children, they're too arrogant for their own
good. They think they're helping science, chasing giant ants.
No respect... Mindless I tell you, just totally mindless."
Jared was furiously winking at me and we almost
burst into the most offensive of laughters when the ship
called to ask how we are doing and would we like
to get picked up and join in the entomologist fun.

And right in that moment, right in the middle of a brilliant
morning swelling with jubilant noises, with the energy of life
that was floating all around us, with the sadness of the past
momentarily buried, with uncountable years ahead of us still,
and with our futures always, forever uncertain, we had nothing
left, but to join in,
                        and do our best in everything we endeavour,
pick ourselves up, let paradise into our hearts, and move on.

The Ambiguous Politics of Unrooted/Unrouted Aesthetics and the (Ex-)Temporal Discontinuance of Demise in the Poetry of Jared Q. I. Vile

by F. J. Bloownt

How does one analyse prewar writing in a boring post-war context in which the audience has grown meek, cow-like and excessively pacifist so it can no longer relate to and inhabit the jarring upheaval of the war? Does one not? Or does one swerve left and right to find a road across the do-good peace-blather-peace monotony and reach the brutality and dissolution of the real which is always simultaneously unreal as well? These are difficult questions that also pose themselves on a purely epistemological level; pragmatically bound individuals might find themselves theoretically underfunded should they attempt to cross the ultra-confusing boundaries of prewar times, warfare intensity and multiple contemporaneity aftermaths. A longing for war and destruction has planted itself deep into human nature many millions of years ago, most probably as the first tool-using humans began to fight and maim and kill each other over gain, be that interpersonal, territorial, resource-related or any other gain. We have always competed, and will do so forever, while war is the ultimate expression of our own darkest desires for dominance, control, power and the subjugation of others like us into systems of hierarchy and order. Some would quote the fact that our current historical moment is one of peace that has lasted for centuries, but that does not change the devastating nature of the human. The "homo sapiens" identity is, ultimately and inevitably, death, so bringing the process of death unto others can only be a constant expression and re-expression of that ultimate identity. I, of course, do not enjoy this given in the least, but must bow down to the nature of the unreal reality that we are subjects of, that drives us to push the tangible of the body towards the (un)reality of its death.

Our own diversity mirrors the total fragmentation of the unreal reality (or should I call it the real unreality?) and the natural identity (death) of the human. We will certainly look for the made identity of the human as well, the unreal real and real unreal of culture, although we will certainly find that the core and bottom line of such is, once again, termination, a process and a state as well, always in simultaneity. Most important, however, is the text that builds all of this. Researchers spend lifetimes trying hard to read and interpret and learn and unlearn and write that text (for which unlearning is of course required). The text represents, ontologically, both a bridge and a shoreline to the release of the world through itself. It revolves in natural cycles, just like time which has, rather confusingly, been dubbed yet another dimension by physicists, and uses the author and the reader and the critic (the first two of which always awkwardly swap roles) as conduits for deferring the meaning of both the life before death and the self which is itself (time/text/self identity) and its manifestation. Having said that, I must also irrevocably acknowledge that the author is dead – always has been, always will be. This was clear already to the critics of the very distant awakening of textual deconstruction within the intersectionalities of the promiscuously isolable concurrent contemporaneities of the 20th century. The author has no business staying alive, both as a text and as a death. In the eternally recurring mode of war, the author may not retain any so-called, purely fictional free will due to the ethical imperative towards the text: the reading must be free and the interpretation must be unchained so that the writing of bodies, selves, identities, cultures and (re-)textualisations in the endless cycles of time, text and history can proceed unimpeded. The person of the author cannot be relevant when the author must be dead for the freedom of the (re-)interpreter to exist in the first place; the desire, deep within the human, towards domination and war and destructive control (constantly dissolving and re-solving) cannot be extricated from the under/writing of the text and the cycle as main "self" elements of forever.

These deliberations may seem a tad too abstract but they are in good agreement with many examples we can easily observe. The current poetry collection, subject of this essay as well, does not constitute an exception to the rule: Jared Vile is literally dead at the moment his text(s) reaches us and we can read and re-write the connections to the megatext/s of our existence at ease. Be that as it may, I must lodge a protest against prewar scaremongers: wars always start. No matter if we warn others and point to ominous signs or horizons of impending doom, war is inevitable as the cycle of time and text. I experienced this first-hand as a child, a little over five and a quarter centuries ago, in the middle of the Second Systemwide Sol War (also designated the Last Humanity War by some unbelievably starry-eyed idealists) when my mother had to work any odd space-habitat job to feed us during the Saturn campaigns, and later as well, when the fighting spread in the interstellar space towards and beyond Alpha Centauri. The memories of the broken people I saw as a child and a young man can only confirm the inevitability of human devastation, whatever the surreal optimists of today might try to convince us of. The charred limbs, the impossibly but intriguingly twisted bodies and the hugely diverse losses of minds and souls haunt my digestion to this day and never fail to both send some proverbial shivers down my spine and remind me to chastise the scaremongers wherever and whenever I may find them.

The rather minor literary figure of Jared Vile does possess the vital features of war scaremongers and as such is of interest to all scholars of the period. Historians will surely find some parallels between his writings and the much larger events that swept the phase of the historical cycle he lived through. What is of interest to me, though, is the double unconsciousness, if I can conceivably call it that, of the prewar warner and the run-of-the-mill aestheticist. The second personality in this multiple-personality order displays itself prominently from the very beginning. Texts like "There Is No You" and "Interaction Is", more specifically the last one with its preposterous rhyming – which, by the way, seems to be a hallmark of a kind of Vile's version of an early period – signify an invertedly dishonest desire for control that is not "control". Furthermore, this is clearly visible even in pieces that seem incomplete and/or too complete and self-rhymingly-enclosed but are placed in otherwise interesting cycles, such as "The Diesel Kids", "Irresistible Drive", "Calling God Tonight Blues", the utterly pink "Crisp Waters" and

"The Fastest Ever"; or in cycles that are "interesting" for all the wrong reasons, examples under this category being "Another One for the Purple (Colour of Your Eyes)", "First Binding", "The Devil Works", "What Cannot Do Us in", "The Censor Outside", etc., etc. Vile has underdone the destructive sexual desires and overtones in this textuality in order to present a palatable identity to the waiting public of the prewar period with a clear wish for attention and acceptance as tell-tale features and signs of a mundane-personality-(dis)order-in-hiding. I am not saying there is something wrong with that, I am rather saying that the breakage of the internal self due to compounded pressures from within, without and other dimensions results almost always, with very few unpredictable exceptions, in a confused aesthetics lacking roots and routes. And what can be a bigger and more delicious crime as well as a perfectly human expression of the text and its identity in the unreality of the real than that? In a sense, one does not even need to know anything about the author to comprehend this simple fact. The way things look, no one will ever have full access to any remaining documentation – or to any detailed information whatever – on Jared Vile's biographical, political and cultural particularities. Let me be clear about this then: no one really ever *needs* that information to read and re-write. Some of the texts that I mentioned above, like "You Won't", "Calling God Tonight Blues" and "Breaker of Circles", resemble song lyrics and seem to border on the laughable, but that is precisely where the enjoyment of the destructive human nature can be had at maximum in a mode of Schadenfreudian reading and writing along. I can only add that we are all authors as well – and we are all quite dead (in several senses).

The state and process of death cannot nonetheless prevent us from producing and supplying hard evaluative stances towards what we insist on designating "art production". The poetry (let us call it that) of Jared Vile does not add anything new to poetry itself but is rather interesting to read psychologically due to its many eigenstates of (bizarre) style and its re-/treading of multiple genre tropes, specifically those of science fiction. One can observe these fundamental trademarks of Vile's, somewhat intermittently, from the very opener of this current volume to the last lines of the closing prose-rhythm exercise. "The Eyes That Hold the Gentle

Books", "A Mystery Link", "Crisp Waters", the more blatant love lyricism of "The Fastest Ever", "The Confession and the Explanation" and "Egotistical Paramour Comparativism", but also "Reemuv-Lha's New Vampires", "Past the Layered Stones" (incomprehensible science fiction since Venus was not deemed terraformable in his lifetime [and by the way, could we really have annihilated lifeforms by terraforming Venus? some would answer in the affirmative]) and the grandly clumsy "grand finale" of "Those Mindless Tourists" (just as incomprehensible as the previous one, we all know there are no such hyperfast spaceships) showcase a removal from the unavoidable war brutality of the reality-unreality twin that can only be the product of an unbelieving make-believe. Still, the tropes are followed closely, there is invention, there is a bit of warmed-up intrigue and sandy emotion, ideas are extended towards their illogical conclusions (as in all of infantile science fiction), and so on, and so forth. Poems like "Spilt for the Children" and "Inside Looking Out" demonstrate differently accented sensibilities and quite probably the very few valuable and redeeming qualities of these early works (since that is what they presumably but rather undoubtedly are). Several texts move more ostensibly into territories of horror and other indefinable fantasy writings, such as "Newly Posted", "Killed Him", "The Shivers" and "The Devil Works". The collection as a whole and the spreading of science fictions, horrors and other fantasies among its constituent cycles reveals an invisible lack of reconciliation with the death fundament. It is extraordinarily difficult to draw psychological conclusions from this type of high-spread, low-density textual exercises, though one could postulate a certain arrogance and confusion in the larger scale of the work as envisaged and hierarchically ordered. Particularly noteworthy for its presumptuousness is the science fiction of the already listed ending which does not seem to find anything aesthetically pleasing or reflective of its both historical and fictional circumstances to write home about. At a similar or even higher level of human hubris one can find the texts in the entire sections ""Too Much Love"" and "The Four Siblings": they do not even attempt to listen to the circular motions of the self, the history and the body/identity duality in the basic human mode of dying and death, let alone come to terms with desire and war as ultimate drives in the homo sapiens conundrum of continuing existence. Is Jared Vile attempting to discontinue death, killing and destruction via mere words? If he were a contemporary, we might wish him good luck, stand back and enjoy the peculiar show that would follow. I will leave aside the poisonous idea of writing so-called "love poems"; even the supposedly political moves in some texts could be outright cringeworthy to the experienced members of my generation. Signs of cowardly armchair politics instead of meditations on the ineluctabilities of the human can be found in "love poems" such as "First Binding" and "One Condition Away" as well as, way more prominently, in the openly politically critical "The University of Anger" and "If This World Teaches You", in "For a Piece of Contact", "Gigachiroptera Sapiens Reforming", "Dear Old Bear (A Letter to a Prisoner)" and, finally and most unbelievably, "Fissure and Flux". Mr Vile sees himself as a cleansing agent and a revolutionary (the link to the conspiracy theories will be briefly discussed below) who has set himself the goal to save us all from war and pain. Ah, the pure hauteur of the youth: so quickly silenced by the advances of age, suffering, war and doom.

I guess, all of the preceding notwithstanding, that this could simply be the only way to peddle war scaremongering in times of upcoming crisis. It is ultimately and always better to simply accept the juncture of warfare and its devastations as inevitable and concentrate on the cyclical re-doings of identity and time than to waste time on "preventative measures". The diversity of poetry on display here, poetry focusing on those desperate and thus mildly entertaining measures, once again, mirrors human social and individual fragmentation whatever the poet might say. One relatively ancient critic (I need not name him – those who know him know the quote as well) was right to insist that poets know nothing, least of all their poetry and the ways in which it comes to life to be safely killed and prepared in its demise for the preservation of the printed or digital page. As they said in ancient Teutonic, to der Ziege(l)führer to show a middle finger, anyone can do that; the cosmic difficulty lies in the sufferance of suffering and death in their equally cosmic certainty. As a great poet and our contemporary who passed away into the textual void not so long ago, Alfrothul Blankoleerensee, often remarked, we frequently feel the paralysis in the mirror of the twins of pain (meaning death and suffering and all their infinite self-versus-other reflexions), but just as frequently fail to emote or comprehend, or let alone truly express, this paralysis in our existence. The sometimes amusing products of this failure can be encountered all over the universe of humanity.

Jared Vile's science fiction/political/love execrations constitute, once again, no exception to this cardinal rule. He seems to have taken his heiliger Zwischenstuhl (both because it is holy to the texter himself in all his forms, and because its implications are rather common and commonly well understood [for those who are failing to follow: we all produce myriad types of Stuhl and often one variety inserts itself between others, hence my metaphor]) and positioned its bits and pieces "strategically" to influence the minds of the susceptible believers, all, of course, to no avail at all. As such, he cannot be or, more precisely, cannot have been the famed "revolutionary" Joseph Astas Kir Demeter in any imaginable manner. Besides, there have been numerous scientific examinations of similar claims throughout the past four centuries and they have disproved any possible relationship between the two based on the hard sciences of facial recognition, graphology and DNA analysis, among others. (The most likely candidate for Demeter's fame is one Dardanus Djadjaliningrat.) An imaginary link to a long dead political figure of some infamy is not the intriguing facet of Vile's collection. Loss, depression and their poetic depictions rank as the most interesting elements in a book otherwise earmarked by convulsive denials of the real-unreal's cyclical inevitabilities. To paraphrase another ancient political figure, Ioseb Besarionis dze Jughashvili, the deaths of billions are always statistics, but the death of one is an impossible tragedy. This is where Jared Vile shines, albeit briefly, as a thinker and poet. Even the science fictional inclinations do not detract from his visions of dear lives cut and lost; "Spilt for the Children" is a case in point here, despite its ending pushing towards the future: the ending is in truth an empty promise and thus reverberates perfectly within the hollow human fundaments of death and pain. Some of the "love" poems such as "Always Already Insufficient" and even "Egotistical

Paramour Comparativism", as well as the existential question/uncertainty mirror "Monument to a Child Fast Asleep", hint at a serious attempt at grappling with the usual dread before the deadly basis of cyclical (un)reality. Jared Vile was no "revolutionary" but a man who understood, at least minimally, pain and loss, and the best indication of that is the cycle "Crossing the Wall". The very structure of this precisely ordered piece is at peace with the cycles of identity, history, death and destiny, and unveils its suffering proudly, wearing it on its poetical sleeve. In fact, I would venture the opinion that one could read only the last four or five poems I mentioned in this analysis and gain the best from the collected works of Jared Q. I. Vile: because one does definitely not need to read until the end of a given text, or read absolutely all its parts (in case of a collection), to know everything about it. I certainly did not; any other approach is completionist and goes radically and uselessly against the fragmented nature of the human. Text, in general and in principle, is always and forever an incomplete and in-becoming basis of the real-unreal duality; as such, it cannot be comprehended completely, let alone read completely, and anyone who thinks otherwise is a slightly deranged completionist who knows nothing of the cycles of time, self, fate and demise. It is precisely these cycles that Jared Vile has captured, however briefly, in his textual work, and so unveils for us from time to time in this collection our eternally recurring recycling of ourselves and our self-narrativisations that also simultaneously (re-)narrate our histories socially and individually. In the endless loop of time, we shall return to ourselves and our previous textualisations time and again, and again. "Crossing the Wall" demonstrates, at its very end, that death is, in a certain morbid sense, the only escape from this eternally returning loop motion. The vision from a "beyond" the poem paints is the recurring nightmare of pure human madness and its only palpable twin, the utter flight via total demise.

Ferdinand Jebideiah Bloownt
4258.03.34
New Dallas, North America & EC/The Oxbryd, New Europe, Earth

An Afterword about Jared Vile's Life

by A. Vile

My name is Andonia Vile and I am the great-great-granddaughter of Jared Quieton Ilyief Vile. I am partially responsible for the little book you are reading now: it was me who found the manuscript between old books and papers that I wanted to actually recycle. The people who I worked with on this publication, Annique Estelle Arhangelskaya-Ing and Romonu Gev, insisted that I write an afterword. They became good friends during the time it took us to finish the work. They are also excellent professionals and can be very convincing. I thought I'd make them happy, give it a go and write something, but I'm unfortunately not that good with words, so please bear with me.

I am a biochemical constructionist by profession. These days, as you know, we all work with AI colleagues and the workloads are never huge. That makes each job much more fun. My usual tasks include the creation of functional composite molecules based on organic and quasi-organic designs for various nano-level applications, so I spend a lot of time inside 4-d plotters and simulations. This has made something of an artist out of me over the years: I regularly work on the side to create functioning, "posable" objects, and as you might've guessed, their structures and functions are often based on my biochemical constructions. My creative works are few in number. A couple of friends call them "kinetic sculptures" and I like that although I know it's an archaic description. What's important in the entire thing is that I like to work visually and I prefer to explore all the available angles, connections and freedoms of movement.

Maybe that's what pushed me to turn all those old cartons upside down and sift through their contents. I don't like to leave angles unexplored and so I more often than not find interesting connections between an object's parts, or between different objects. This time, though, I found something that really stumped me. The moment I realised what it was, I was sure I wanted to publish my great-great-grandfather's manuscript, the problem was what to do with his diary. You see, that fat old notebook contains quite a lot of sad and painful personal stories. Not only was he ill with what doctors at the time called hypermelanoma, he was also trying to help all his poor relations and at the same time work on his creative projects and engage with the bigger political problems. The situation was very chaotic. One man in the extended family had even become something of a petty thief because he was so extremely poor and uneducated, and was an embarrassment to everyone. All that took its toll on Jared during the years he wrote in the diary. It's strange, I read the everyday thoughts of a distant relative and it all feels like it happened 20 years ago, not 13 centuries ago, no matter how different and strange his words sound now. The good thing I'm constantly reminded of is that no one today must live the lives of poverty that Jared's relations had back then. Yes, I know there are people who try such lives of deprivation willingly these days, but they always return to society after a while. Nothing is imposed on them from the outside or by forces they can't control. So it's all research, you go and try an extreme life of poverty just to understand what it's like, how it makes you ill physically, how it crushes your spirit. That I understand. But I still don't want to bring the information in that journal into the open because it's so painful. Maybe some day I'll sit down with good friends and professionals like Annique and Romonu and select parts of it for publishing, or maybe friendly historians will agree to read parts of it without publishing or directly quoting what they read. We'll see.

I really don't know how Jared would have reacted to any of this. I have of course never met him and know little about him. All of my knowledge, all of my information comes from my grandparents. My grandfather Runomo and his sisters told me basically all the stories I can remember about him. My grandfather's sisters died when I was still a child though and I remember them very vaguely. My grandfather Runomo, on the other hand, lived for a very long time, he died about 30 years ago, and he tried to find an hour or two to tell me a couple of stories every time we met. I'm really grateful to him for that, I feel that he gave me something massive and important, a family history if you want, to keep safe for the future with myself and the other relatives

– and the children of course. So here I'd like to tell you three very short stories about Jared Vile because I think they helped me understand some of his confusing poetry. They might help you as well.

The first story is about a musical project he was taking part in. The friends of his who were working with him on it wanted to have the thing finished very quickly, but Jared wasn't a professional musician like them. He was a good poet though and composed almost all of the lyrics. That's when things went wrong and Jared had to leave. He simply had way too many personal problems and family troubles at the time to be able to improve himself musically. What he did was odd: he destroyed all his lyrics, deleted the files, burnt all the printouts. He said that he can recreate all of them from memory if they truly mattered, if there was a real vibe to them. My grandfather never told me the names of those musician friends, he probably didn't know them either, but he always told me that Jared rewrote everything from scratch and made it into something else, not lyrics. I didn't know whether to believe that, but the diary I found confirms all of it. The remade lyrics are unfortunately missing. I tried to find them and a couple of other things the journal mentions, with no luck at all, so maybe the Ultracontinentals destroyed much more than people know. They were a real bunch, the Ultracons.

Speaking of them, the second story is about Jared and an Ultracon hit team of sorts. He was neither openly nor secretly attacked with physical violence because he was a public figure, but the Ultracons had invented a tactic to discredit such people: they gathered prominent intellectuals and academics on their side and arranged them in teams that spat out all possible kinds of barely legal abuse on their victims. They performed what people usually call character assassinations by badgering and heckling their targets in the flesh, in media, on-line or any other way they could. As my grandfather Runomo told me, this didn't faze my great-great-grandfather very much. In the journal, he mentions these people in passing and refers to them as "my hit squad" or "my personalised assassins". You know that the usual Ultracon philosophy said no man is an island, but all men are huge, separated continents and must survive in the jungle of the universe on their own to prove their worth. The Ultracons never knew how right they were about my great-great-grandfather. He took in all the insults of his personalised hit squad and didn't bat an eyelash, not once. My grandfather told me that Jared used to say: better swallow an ugly insult than commit a crime when you try to respond in kind or avenge yourself. The insult one can transform creatively later, but the crime stays a crime whatever you do afterwards. In the end, the hit squad attacks didn't matter much, although they continued after Jared was arrested and then released from jail. The war finally made such tactics obsolete because it introduced martial law and the Ultracons could do whatever they wanted with their opponents. That almost completely silenced my great-great-grandfather as well.

The last story I'd like to tell you is precisely about Jared's time in jail and the circumstances which led to that episode. In early 2933, the Ultracons won a powerful majority in the European parliament at the elections. For the first time, they didn't need any coalitions to make their policies into law. One of the first laws they passed then was to seriously increase military budgets across the board. A lot of people on all sides protested because they thought the decision to syphon money off into the military will harm all other sectors after the recent pharmaceutical and bank crises. The history books have a much better overview of this period, I'm just summarising quickly. Jared was one of the people who protested most loudly against this, he was at all the rallies, spoke to the press and wrote several pieces, did everything he thought he could. One demonstration he was at towards the end of spring that year turned violent and he got arrested with everyone else. The courts were instructed to proceed as fast as possible with the sentencing, so he was basically expedited into jail with a two-year sentence in virtually no time and with very little of what is called due process. He didn't give up though and mounted a combined appeal and defence as a sort of class-action counter-suit. I don't really know the precise legal terminology for this, so please don't consider me rude and look up the details for yourselves if you want to. The gist of the matter was that he pushed against the Ultracon system on its own grounds. He had the idea to argue that the protests and all his public objections had as their aim only the well-being and improvement of the supra-state. The Ultracons declared the exact same goal. Jared's self-defence group used their time in jail to prepare some economic statistics and show that all sorts of catastrophic consequences were quite probable as a result of the highly increased military spending. The courts agreed and set the entire group free after four months, overturning their sentences. Higher instances agreed with that ruling as well. What's more, several months later some of the things the group had pointed to using statistics started happening. Agricultural production went down very badly, crime increased in a strange correlation with decreases in sports and arts spending that no one could explain and the transportation systems across the supra-state suffered. The entire crisis wasn't as disastrous as the little defence group had predicted but developed in a very similar way to what they had warned about. They got together again and decided to counter-sue the government for damages, and won sometime in the harsh winter of 2935. There were appeals, and the awarded damages were reduced, and so on, but the result stayed the same. My great-grandmother Flouera, mother of my grandfather Runomo, was in her late teens when the episode began in 2933 and remembered it all very vividly. I never heard the story from her, I was still a baby when she died, but she wrote every detail down in her diary and told and re-told the tale as she had experienced it many times to anyone who would listen, family or not. Jared's journal has very few details on this and mostly refers to his so-to-say political diary, but that's not very important in this case. I find this piece of his history very telling.

Finally, no one can actually say with certainty if he did transform into the famous revolutionary Joseph Demeter after he disappeared in late 2942. He could have really had plastic surgery and vocal cord re-arrangements and so on. I don't find it possible that Dardanus Djadjaliningrat was Joe Demeter – Dardanus was a well-known revolutionary in his own right, plus he was a shorter black man, he had both Indian and African ancestors. My great-great-grandfather was a fairly tall white guy, just like Joe D., and his family came from what was called Eastern Europe in earlier centuries. I sat down and read some history about the period and about Joseph Demeter. To my untrained mind, there are few similarities between Joe D. and the Jared Vile that I now know from his diary. The poetry says otherwise. Poems like "The University of Anger", "If This World Teaches You", "Fissure and Flux" and "Dear Old Bear" tell me that there was an angry man somewhere deep inside my great-great-grandfather. They were all hand-written on paper with lots of corrections, as if he was writing at speed. The paper on which "Dear Old Bear" was written was also different from all other materials I found in the small strongbox. Could he have written that poem while he was still in prison? Could he have decided to leave everything behind and fight back as a guerrilla? But then how could he just simply go away in the middle of the war and abandon his family? A revolutionary with a good plan or a man who provides for his nearest and dearest people – that was a very tough choice if he really did have to make it. His wife and two of his five children died shortly after the war, in the chaos. Flouera remembered very clearly how one of her brothers succumbed to an illness, and later her mother and older sister disappeared. Their bodies were discovered in the rubble of an ammunition dump explosion a week after that. If Jared had been with them, he would have been most probably unable to prevent any of that horror. But in the other case, if he had been out there, organising and fighting, things would also have been no different. So I'd like to believe that he really was that revolutionary. I want to believe that he fought hard against the Ultracons and gave them hell. It's very very likely that I will never know, but I want to believe that a man like my great-great-grandfather Jared Vile could do something profound for this world, and that people would remember him fondly for it.

Thank you for reading this book and my little afterword, and sorry if I've rambled on and maybe bored you with my old stories. I'm very glad that I found this small piece of legacy and that I was able to work with good people to bring it into the light.

Andonia Vile
4258.03.17
New Hellven, Mars

Addendum: The Sun's Prayer

by A. E. Arhangelskaya-Ing

Less than 25 hours ago, I received an urgent message from Andonia Vile. For the past two or three weeks, something inexplicable had bothered her about the strongbox she found and eventually made her take a closer look at it. She placed it into a simple industrial-grade CT scanner and was, once again within the past year, hugely surprised: upon closer examination, the strongbox was revealed to have a well-disguised false bottom. That additional container-within-the-container proved difficult to open because it was brazed/soldered in several places. The construction seems to have been created with the intent to make it as permanent and as sturdy as possible. Inside, Andonia found three pages of a hand-written poem. Quick but thorough handwriting (UDE) and paper material chemical analyses prove that this is another poem by Jared Q. I. Vile. Furthermore, the poem's text is better preserved than others in the manuscript, while the writing is clean, orderly and devoid of markings or corrections, thus obviously not a first draft. Since our project was already allocated production machines and time, I persuaded Andonia and Romonu to append this poem as an addendum to the book. They objected that the nature of the poem and the potential historical significance of the information it contains may perhaps be better served if revealed to the public later, in a better-understood scientific context and as a well-integrated part of the book. Unfortunately, that would have meant delaying the book's release by more than a year (perhaps even two or three years, depending on production availabilities). Additionally, the impact of the revelation may have been drowned in loud debates, especially in the spheres of historical, political, literary and cultural analysis. These arguments prevailed and I was able to convince my work partners that an immediate release could be the best option we have under the current circumstances. Should I happen to be proved wrong, I assume full responsibility for any unpleasant or damaging consequences. Despite all of this, I find that this last poem – probably the very last one by Jared Vile anyone will ever discover – comes as a final, reassuring sign of certainty and clarity in the long and frequently surprising story of his unparalleled life.

> *Annique Estelle Arhangelskaya-Ing*
> *4258.05.02*
> *Versta Chi, Kepler 512 D-8*

The Sun's Prayer

Oh Sun, you shining, burning Sun, you mighty Sun, my Star,
I see you in the sky, oh Sun, shining over houses every morning,
throwing light on roads and burning over hills and fields and cities,
illuminating forests, oceans, souls and minds; and
with your yellow hands, you mighty Sun, I see you
holding mountains down!

Shine on you brightest Star of mine, over bridges, over lakes,
burn brightly over deserts, over valleys, over seas;
but hide behind a cloud awhile, burn not my love
for she is toiling in this broken world from dawn till dusk,
and she is my true South on every day and night, hands hard at

work

to keep the small ones fed and warm,

so hide awhile behind a cloud, oh burning mighty Sun,
don't burn her mind to cinders; let my love rest, oh scorching Sun!
And grant me shade and silence and a path
to fight the war that I have chosen, searing Sun,
and give me strength like all the fires in your heart
to keep the promises I've spoken, and survive, oh Sun.

For my face is now another's, and my blood is now
forever changed, oh mighty Sun, transformed I am
under your singeing gaze into myself but not myself

to struggle for the futures I have seen inside your eye
and heart, my Star of fire and of glory. Like you, from far away
I'll watch my children grow and then grow old, oh Sun,

like you, I've chosen not to touch again,
or the very surface of my skin may burn the ones I love.
So grant me liquid lava in my veins, oh mighty Sun,
so I can need no rest and no respite in all the years
of the heavy work ahead, and grant me courage, burning Sun,
and grant me will so I will strike with soul and spirit

the murderers and slavers in your realm, oh mighty Sun.
Shine on, my Star of glory and of fire,
shine on through mornings, noons and eves,
and keep your searing eye upon my love and our little children,
keep them safe within your mighty light,
keep the tears from my heart in the silence of your holy flames,

and keep my soul high-armoured in your molten metal
so it will never falter, never hesitate to forge ahead,
and keep my mind as sharp as all the flames inside you,
so with you by my side, in the names of everyone I love and
                                                    cherish,
I'll rise with millions in truest fires of equality and freedom,
oh brightest Star, oh burning, searing, scorching mighty Sun!

Acknowledgements

I would like to thank:

My mother, father and sister, for their love and their support in every way imaginable; that's one debt of gratitude I'll never be able to repay.

My good friends, for everything. Among them: Jonas & Verena Kyratzes, for way too many things to enumerate here; Senta Sanders and Beate Greisel, for letting me rant, listening carefully and giving me brilliant sparks of thought in response; Sara Heristchi, for reading me with a constructive, critical and very very friendly eye; Plamen Ivanov and Rossitsa Kaltcheva, for talking about all the important stuff, on many separate occasions, over a couple of beers. To paraphrase that old song, we all do get by with a little help from our friends.

You, the reader, for reading my book. Thank you for your support. I really appreciate it!

And last but unquestionably not least, the art that enables us to believe. As Babylon 5 puts it: Faith Manages.

Ivaylo R. Shmilev
2016.12.20
Frankfurt am Main, Germany, Earth

PS If you'd like to contact me for any reason - to share your impressions, let me know about a review you've written on your favourite site, request a review copy if you're a journalist, invite me for a reading and so on - please use this information.

Website: http://ivoshmilev.net/
Twitter: https://twitter.com/iv0rshmilev
Facebook: https://www.facebook.com/IvoShmilev

Made in the USA
Columbia, SC
06 July 2017